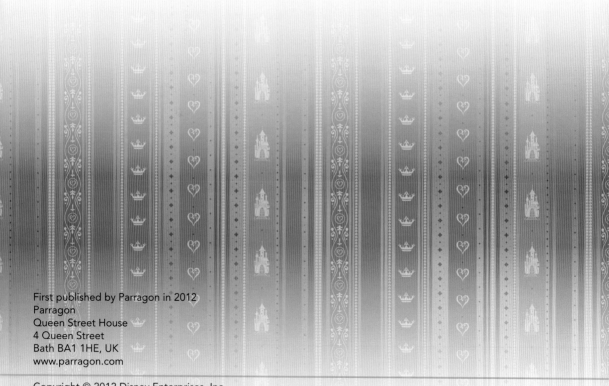

First published by Parragon in 2012
Parragon
Queen Street House
4 Queen Street
Bath BA1 1HE, UK
www.parragon.com

Edited by: Katrina Hanford
Designed by: Pete Hampshire
Production by: Emma Fulleylove

ISBN 978-1-4454-6502-9

Printed in China

Enchanting Magical Stories

Contents

Tiana's Royal Wedding

After many adventures, Tiana and Naveen were getting married! Together they welcomed Naveen's parents, the King and Queen, to New Orleans for the wedding.

And all too soon the royal helpers cornered
Tiana, announcing their plans for her wedding.
  "We'll do this… and this… and this," they told
her. Tiana's head was spinning!

"Dress!"   *"Dinner!"*

"Cake!"

"I don't want to upset the King and Queen, but their royal helpers' wedding plans aren't right for me!" Tiana told her friend Charlotte.

"It's your wedding! You should do what you want," Charlotte said.
So Tiana made her first wedding decision: she asked Charlotte to be her maid of honour!

Just then, Tiana's mother walked in. "I'd like to make your dream gown for you," she said.

"Oh, Mama! That's perfect!" Tiana smiled when she saw Eudora's sketch.

Prince Naveen and Louis secretly planned the music for the wedding reception.

"The royal helpers will choose boring music," Naveen told Louis. "The perfect music should be jazzy and romantic. It should make Tiana feel like dancing!"

And after everyone else had gone to bed, Tiana sneaked into the kitchen to work on the menu with Charlotte.

"I want a taste of New Orleans," Tiana said as she began working. "Let's start with gumbo."

17

Just before bed, Charlotte said, "Tia, every bride needs something old, something new, something borrowed and something blue. So here's your 'something blue'."
She handed Tiana a beautiful blue necklace.

The next day, Tiana faced the royal helpers.
"Thank you for helping," Tiana said, "but I already have everything I need."

Though surprised, they agreed – Tiana should have her dream wedding!

Just then, the Queen of Maldonia walked into the room. Tiana looked at her nervously. Would she be angry with the wedding plans Tiana had made?

"Tiana dear, I am glad you are planning the wedding you want, but would you do me the honour of wearing the tiara I wore when I wed the King?" The Queen gently placed the tiara on Tiana's head.

Soon, it was time for the final fitting
of Tiana's wedding gown. It was stunning, and
best of all, she could feel her mother's love in
every stitch.

Everything seemed perfect. But Tiana missed her
father. The night before the wedding, as she gazed at
the Evening Star – and its new twinkling companion,
her firefly friend Ray – Tiana realized her father would
always be part of her.

The next day, Big Daddy walked Tiana
down the aisle. Inside her bouquet, she carried
her father's favourite **old** spoon. She wore her
new gown from Eudora, the tiara **borrowed** from
the Queen and Lottie's **blue** necklace
under her veil.

As Naveen and Tiana kissed,
she knew that love was what
made her wedding – and her
life – perfect. She and Naveen
were now *husband* and *wife*...

...and **_prince_** and **_princess_** of Maldonia!

All of New Orleans turned out
for their *first* appearance...

...and their *first* dance.

The wedding guests enjoyed Princess Tiana's cooking. And as Tiana and Naveen took the first nibble of their made-with-love cake, they shared the sweetness of their new life *together.*

Belle's Royal Wedding

*B*elle's wedding was just days away. "I'm so happy!" Belle told Mrs Potts. "The Prince has done so much for me. I want to make our wedding a special celebration. We need to show him how much we appreciate him, and how well-loved he is."

"What a wonderful idea, my dear!" said Mrs Potts.

Belle thought back to when she first arrived at the castle. It was so frightening – everyone was under a magical spell. The Prince had become an angry Beast and the servants were enchanted objects.

But over time, Belle became friends with
the staff. Then she and the Beast fell in
love and the spell was broken. The whole
household became a family.

Belle smiled at her friends. "It will mean so much
to him to have you all there!" she said. "I know you
all want to help with the preparations, but you must
also help by being our guests."

Mrs Potts and the other servants worked hard to prepare for the big day.

They were determined that the couple feel *love* in every detail.

Meanwhile, the Prince was preparing for the wedding, too.

"I am the happiest man in the world!" he declared to Lumiere and Cogsworth. "And I want Belle to be the happiest woman!"

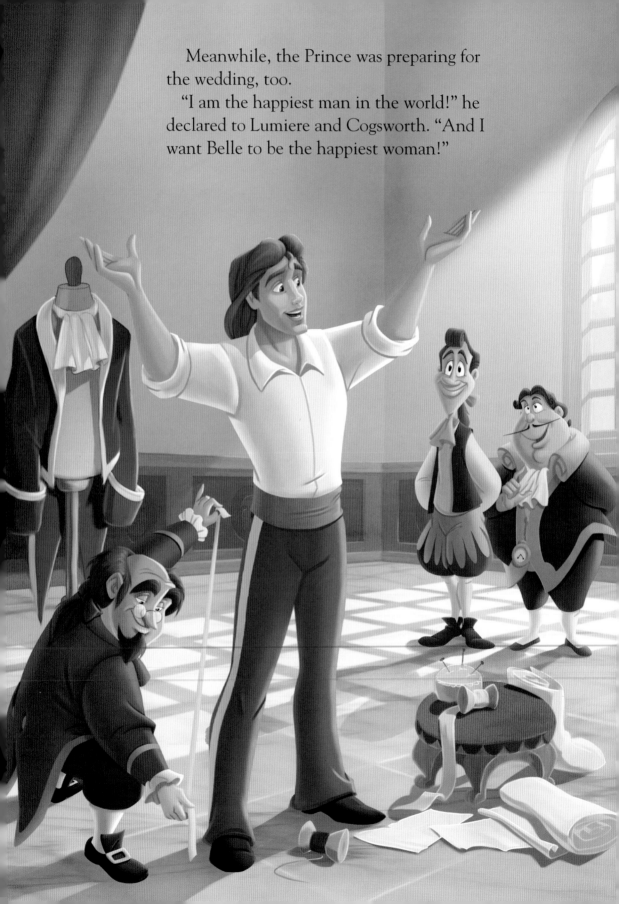

The Prince fell silent as he remembered meeting Belle. Back then, he thought that she could never love a hideous Beast.

But Belle spent time getting to know the Beast. Later on, she chose to return to the castle – and to him – when she could have left forever.

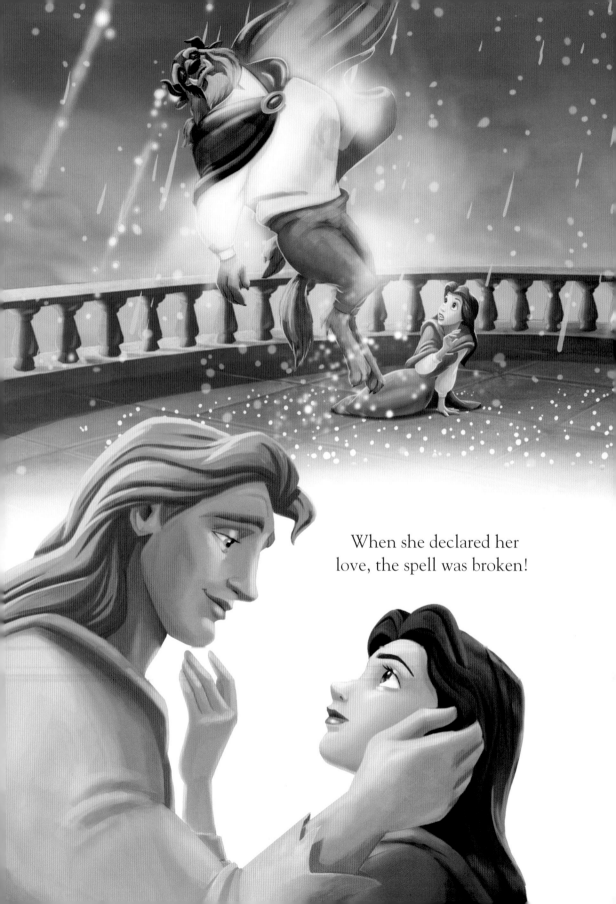

When she declared her
love, the spell was broken!

"How can I show Belle how much I love her?" the
Prince asked. "I know! Let's find a special gift for
her in the village!"

Lumiere and Mrs Potts wondered how they could
show their love and appreciation for the young
couple, too.

The Prince visited every shop in the village.
After a careful search, he found a special gift for
Belle. Then he went to the flower shop to order roses.
"They're Belle's favourite," he explained.
Everyone was impressed by the handsome young man
who was so deeply in love.

The wedding day finally arrived! The Prince could not take his eyes off Belle when she appeared at the top of the grand staircase. Maurice beamed as he escorted his daughter down to the Prince.

During the ceremony, Belle read from her favourite book about exciting adventures. "But they don't compare to what I feel every day with you," she told the Prince.

The Prince gave Belle his gift from the
village – a blank journal. "You can fill it with all
the adventures we will have together," he said.

After the ceremony, Belle and the Prince walked into the ballroom. The staff had created a spectacular celebration!

"Thank you!" said Belle. "But there is so much! I'm not sure even our whole household can eat all this food!" she joked.

Mrs Potts and the other servants just smiled,
and showed the couple into the garden...

…where the whole village was waiting to surprise them!

"I took the liberty to invite them, on behalf of the household," said Lumiere.

"It's a magnificent gift!" the Prince exclaimed.
He looked at Belle. "We are truly loved."
"Yes, we are," Belle agreed, beaming.

"Thank you for coming!" the Prince repeated over and over. He couldn't stop smiling. He and Belle both were thrilled to welcome everyone into their home. When the couple shared their first dance, a shout went up from the crowd. "Congratulations!"

As fireworks lit up the night sky, Belle and the Prince knew that their wedding had been a perfect celebration – for everyone. With so many friends gathered around them, it had been the most magical day of all.

Rapunzel's
Royal Wedding

*S*pring had sprung and Flynn had a surprise for Rapunzel. Max kept guard and Pascal went along to play. But Flynn wanted to be alone with Rapunzel.

Finally, dusk fell, and Flynn took his chance to jump into a boat with Rapunzel. The lovely night reminded them of times past.

Flynn wanted to propose! He put
his hand in his pocket, but – oops!
He did need Pascal and Max, after all.
They had the ring.

"Will you marry me?" Flynn finally asked Rapunzel.

"Yes," Rapunzel said sweetly.

On their way home,
Rapunzel wanted to tell
everyone their happy news!

The boys from the Snuggly Duckling were delighted. They had been waiting for this wedding for years!

Of course, Attila helped Rapunzel design a cake.

They baked and iced, but
nothing seemed quite right.

But with some extra hard work, Rapunzel and Attila finally created the wedding cake of her dreams!

Of course, there were
floral arrangements.

But it took Tor and a field of natural flowers
to please Rapunzel!

As for ring bearers, the choice was clear:
Maximus and Pascal could not have been
prouder to accept!

When it came time to find a dress, Rapunzel was determined to design her own. She sketched and sketched... but simply could not make up her mind!

The boys tried to help, but their dresses didn't seem right either.

Luckily, the Queen arrived. "Darling," she said. "I want to help you find the perfect dress." And she did!

On the morning of the wedding, bells rang throughout the kingdom. Everyone was excited to see the King and Queen happily riding in the royal coach.

And Max and Pascal were thrilled – until Max
sneezed. The rings flew into the air!

As they raced to catch the
lost rings, the King proudly took
Rapunzel's arm.

Flynn beamed as he saw Rapunzel.
Nobody had any idea of what was
happening with Max and Pascal....

The fact is, Max and Pascal were causing
chaos throughout the kingdom.

Max chased one ring...

...and Pascal chased the other.

Everything was almost perfect... until they crashed into
the tar factory.

Still, Max and Pascal returned to the wedding
just in time!

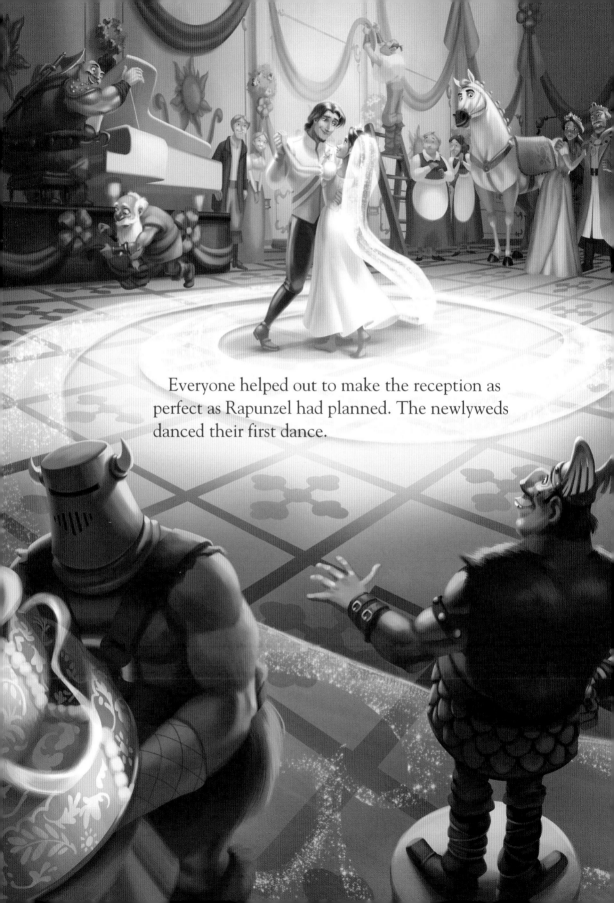

Everyone helped out to make the reception as perfect as Rapunzel had planned. The newlyweds danced their first dance.

They took their first taste of their
wedding cake.

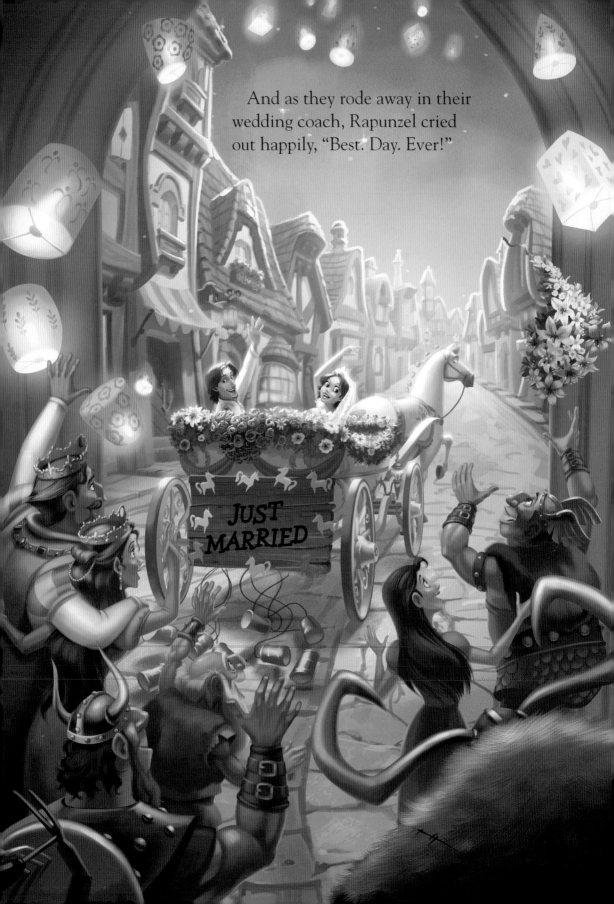

And as they rode away in their
wedding coach, Rapunzel cried
out happily, "Best. Day. Ever!"

Cinderella's
Royal Wedding

*P*rince Charming found the woman he loved. Next he did what all men in love do… He asked, "Will you marry me?" and waited for the answer.

"Cinderelly says yes-yes!"
shouted Gus-Gus.

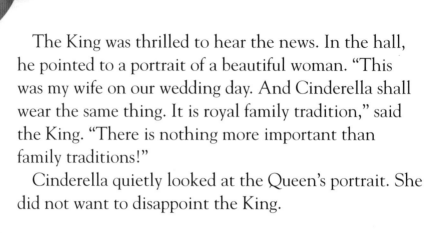

The King was thrilled to hear the news. In the hall, he pointed to a portrait of a beautiful woman. "This was my wife on our wedding day. And Cinderella shall wear the same thing. It is royal family tradition," said the King. "There is nothing more important than family traditions!"

Cinderella quietly looked at the Queen's portrait. She did not want to disappoint the King.

But following this family tradition was not easy with so many royal helpers. Luckily the Grand Duke had a plan.

"Royal traditions – all you need to know," said the Grand Duke, as he brought Cinderella a stack of books.

Cinderella read and read, trying to remember everything until at last she fell asleep.

In the dream, Cinderella's mother gave
her a special gift. "Cinderella my love, this
necklace will remind you that whenever you
have a problem, if you listen to your heart, it
will lead you to the answer."

Cinderella woke up. The dream of her mother filled her with the warmth of love. A smile on her face, she began to search through some of her old trunks.

With the help of her Fairy Godmother, the mice and a little magic, Cinderella found what she was looking for – a portrait of her mother on her wedding day.

Cinderella showed the portrait to the royal dressmaker. "You make such beautiful dresses. Would it be possible for you to help my fairy godmother make me a dress like this?"

The dressmaker bowed his head. "I would be honoured."

Next, Cinderella visited the royal jeweller.
"You are an artist. Do you think it would be
possible to work with my mice friends and
combine two necklaces into one?"

"For you, I shall create the finest necklace
in the Kingdom."

The royal wedding day arrived. The King came to see Cinderella.

"I hope you don't mind. This is a copy of my mother's wedding dress," said Cinderella. "It honours my family tradition. And with my necklace and veil, I also honour yours, your Majesty."

The King saw that his Queen's pearls had been used to make the wedding necklace and veil. "Oh my dear girl, this is a great honour. You have blended the treasures of two families – and created a new tradition for our family."

The King proudly offered Cinderella his arm. "Let's not keep the Prince waiting."

A happy King led Cinderella down the aisle. The guests were thrilled. The Prince was entranced. Even the Grand Duke wiped a tear from his eye.

The Prince and Princess answered the question
that all brides and grooms must answer.
"They do! They do!" shouted Gus-Gus.

The wedding banquet was regal in every detail.

The wedding cake was a work of art.

The bouquet was tossed!

And so, by following tradition – and
her heart – Cinderella had the wedding of
her dreams!

Tiana and the Jewel
of the Bayou

One summer morning, Tiana, Naveen, Eudora and Charlotte were discussing party plans. Tiana's birthday was just days away!

Prince Naveen was worried. Although he had spent weeks looking, he still hadn't found the perfect gift for his princess. And now time was running out!

The prince had looked at everything, from priceless paintings to fine French perfume to beautiful silk and lace.

But he had always come home empty-handed. Nothing seemed special enough for Princess Tiana.

Exhausted, the prince had plopped himself into a chair.

Luckily, the following day, Naveen overheard Tiana speaking with Charlotte in the kitchen.

"When my daddy and I used to go fishing in the bayou, we'd sometimes find a piece of swamp amber," said Tiana. "I thought it was the most precious thing in all the world!"

"That's it!" whispered Naveen, and he dashed out the door.

Naveen met up with the jazz-loving alligator, Louis. The two of them went to ask Mama Odie if she could help them find some swamp amber.

"You don't need my help!" said Mama Odie, laughing. "Go find it yourself. You know what to do."

As the birthday party was about to begin, Tiana
couldn't find Naveen anywhere.

One of the guests said he saw the prince down by the
old, mossy tree in the bayou. Eudora and Charlotte told
Tiana not to worry. But Tiana was afraid Naveen might
be in trouble.

Tiana ran down to the river and
climbed into a rowboat.

As she rowed into the bayou, she saw Naveen in the distance. He was diving into the water at the base of the old tree. Louis was on the bank trying to get a thorn out of his foot.

"Naveen!" Tiana called out. When the prince didn't resurface, she took off her heavy petticoats and dived into the water!

She found Naveen in a tangle
of roots. Tiana grabbed his hand and
pulled him to the surface.

"I was worried about you,"
said Tiana.

Naveen reassured her that
everything was fine and gave her a
hug. Then Tiana and Naveen looked
at each other and laughed. They
were both covered in mud!

Naveen opened his hand to reveal
a plain, muddy rock. "I'm a little
embarrassed," he said. "I was expecting a
sparkling jewel, but this is just..."

"Swamp amber!" Tiana exclaimed.
"What a wonderful birthday surprise!"

When Tiana and Naveen returned to
the party, all the guests gasped at the
sight of them.

Then Charlotte saw the birthday gift and screamed in fright. But Tiana explained that the muddy rock brought back wonderful, loving memories of her daddy. "That is the most precious gift of all," said Tiana. "And now that Naveen is here with me, I couldn't ask for anything more."

As the prince and princess went to change their clothes, Mama Odie picked up the swamp amber.

"A little sparkle couldn't hurt," she said, tossing the rock into a pot of gumbo. "Gumbo, gumbo in the pot, we need some sparkle. What you got?"

In a puff of magic, the swamp amber became a dazzling golden jewel set in a fine necklace.

"Mama Odie!" Naveen exclaimed. "How did you do that?"

Mama Odie winked at Tiana. "Oh, it's just a talent we have down here in the bayou. We like to take things that are a little slimy and rough around the edges and turn 'em into something wonderful!"

Tiana smiled. "Like turning crawfish into gumbo!" she said.

"Or a frog into a prince!" Naveen agreed
as he took his beautiful princess in his arms
and they danced the night away.

Rapunzel and the Jewels of the Crown

*R*apunzel was excited! Freed from her tower and Mother Gothel, she and her friends were travelling back to the kingdom. Soon she would meet her true parents, the King and Queen.

"I can't believe I'm the lost princess," said Rapunzel. "I don't know how to be a princess."

Flynn smiled and said, "You'll be great as a princess. All you have to do is wear a huge, heavy crown...."

"Oh, my!" Rapunzel exclaimed.
"...though it's not a requirement,"
Flynn added quickly.

135

"Let me start over," Flynn said. "Do you remember that tiara from my satchel? Well, let me tell you a story about that."

When I was a kid in the orphanage,
I read a book about the princess and
her tiara. The book said this tiara
symbolized everything the
princess should be.

The tiara's white crystals stood for a strong, adventurous spirit; green represented gentleness and kindness; red stood for courage; and the round golden crown itself stood for leadership.

For years, I thought of that tiara, and then one day, I actually met a gal who could wear it. She certainly was adventurous.

As she travelled towards her dream, she also
showed kindness towards everyone, courage and
definitely leadership. She just seemed to be able to
turn every bad situation into something wonderful!

"Flynn, are you talking about...?"
Rapunzel started.

"You!" Flynn exclaimed. "I'm talking
about all those amazing things you did
when you left your tower in search of those
floating lights."

"But I did all those things when I had long, magical hair!" Rapunzel exclaimed. "Now I can hardly stand up straight. I feel off-balance. I have no idea how to help anyone without magic."

Suddenly they heard a noise above them.
"Nobody move!" someone shouted. Several
men were ready to attack! "Just hand over
your horse!"

Flynn leaped into action, chasing the thieves. "Rapunzel!"
he shouted. "Run away, and don't look back!"

But Rapunzel did not run away. She ran right
into the middle of the fray, trying to rescue
Maximus.

Flynn leaped onto Maximus' back. But
the horse accidentally bucked Flynn off
as he fought against the thieves. Rapunzel
defeated the thieves by herself.

When it was over, Rapunzel scolded the bandits. "It's all my fault," one man replied. "I need your horse to take my son to the doctor."

"Oh, my! Where is he?" Rapunzel asked.

Within minutes, Rapunzel was tending to the boy's injuries. He smiled in relief as he was hoisted onto Maximus for a ride to the Kingdom's doctor.

"How can you ever forgive us?"
the men asked Rapunzel.

Rapunzel thought of the tiara –
adventure, kindness, courage and
leadership. Suddenly, she realized
she didn't need her magical hair.

"Come with me," she said.

At the Kingdom, Rapunzel received her princess crown. But as she waved to the crowds, she knew that no one was as supportive as her faithful new friends! And they always would be, too.

Princesses through the Seasons
Spring

Tiana's Spring Adventure

It was springtime in New Orleans, and time for Mardi Gras!

Tiana and Prince Naveen decided to decorate a float for the big parade. All their friends wanted to help.

But Charlotte had a question: "Who will be the star of this float?"

Everyone had something special to offer.

Charlotte had learned to sew and she made a beautiful costume.

Louis was ready with new songs on his trumpet.

Prince Naveen knew all the latest dance moves.

Then Prince Naveen shook his head.
"Actually," he said. "Tiana should be the star,
because she brought all of us together!"
Tiana laughed. "Me? I'm not a star.
Although I guess I did help bring us
together…"

"...which is why we should *all* be stars on this
float!" she said.

So, on the day of the Mardi Gras parade, all
of them rode on the float. They all shone like
stars and their float was the most magnificent
in the parade!

HOTEL

Rapunzel's Spring Adventure

Rapunzel was having an amazing day. It all started when she met a stranger in her tower. Then she went outside for the first time and now she was running barefoot through the forest!

It was spring, so the flowers were in bloom and everything felt new.

Some of the new things were frightening, though.
At least, they were frightening to Rapunzel.
"It's just a bunny," said Flynn. He was not scared at all.

Rapunzel quickly learned that these forest animals were friendly.

The woods were full of new friends!

Everyone had a wonderful time.

"Oh, my goodness!" Rapunzel cried, as she
burst out of the bushes. "Look at this cute guy.
I had no idea bunnies could grow so big!"
"That's no bunny!" shouted Flynn.

"Then what is he?" Rapunzel asked.

"BEAR!" Flynn yelled. "I mean, TWO BEARS!"

"And they're so nice!" said Rapunzel. "But I feel hungry now. What was the name of that lovely place you promised to take me to? The Snuggly Duckling?"

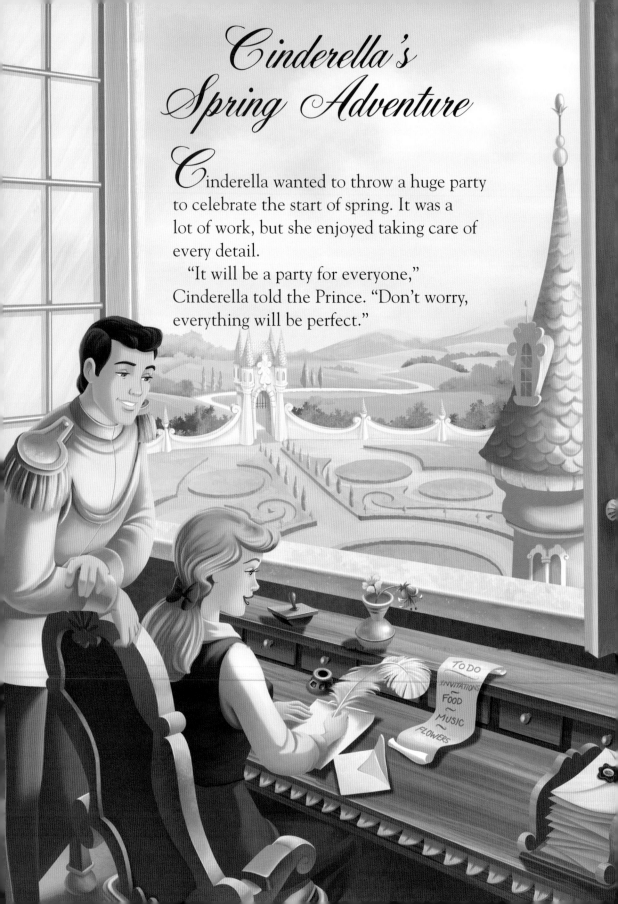

Cinderella's Spring Adventure

Cinderella wanted to throw a huge party to celebrate the start of spring. It was a lot of work, but she enjoyed taking care of every detail.

"It will be a party for everyone," Cinderella told the Prince. "Don't worry, everything will be perfect."

She worked on a special
menu with the royal cook.

She asked the royal
musicians to play music
that would be perfect for
dancing.

And the royal gardener made beautiful flower arrangements.

But as the party was about to begin, Cinderella saw that not all the decorations were set.

"I'm sorry, your highness!" cried the assistant gardener. "My ladder is broken."

Cinderella started to tell him it was fine... but Jaq interrupted. "Don't worry, Cinderelly!" he said. "Leave it to us!"

Jaq, Gus and the birds worked together
quickly to put all the final decorations in place.

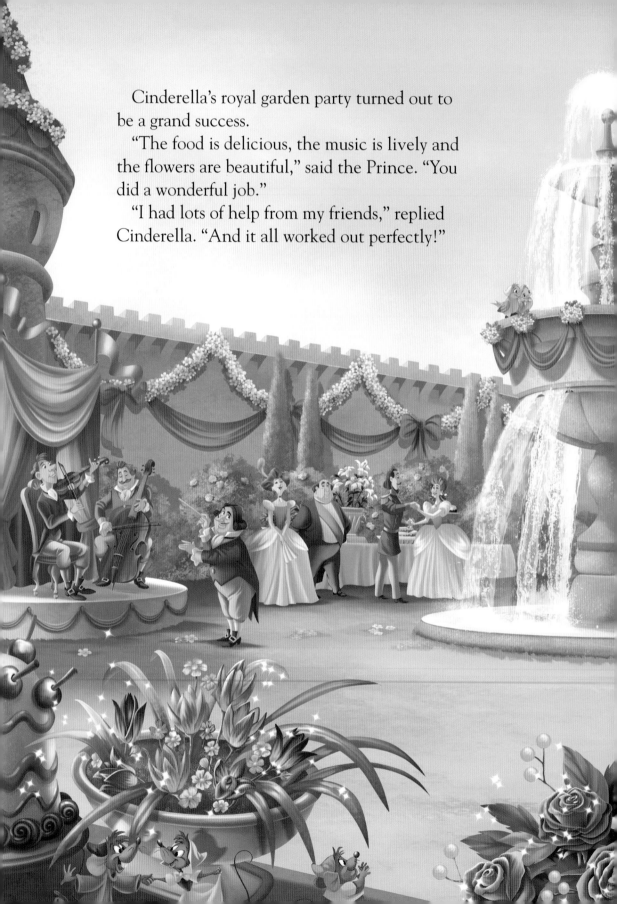

Cinderella's royal garden party turned out to be a grand success.

"The food is delicious, the music is lively and the flowers are beautiful," said the Prince. "You did a wonderful job."

"I had lots of help from my friends," replied Cinderella. "And it all worked out perfectly!"

Sleeping Beauty's Spring Adventure

*O*ne spring morning, in the time before Princess Aurora knew she was a princess, the young woman rowed across the pond with her aunts. Briar Rose, as she was called back then, knew that baby swans had hatched recently, and she wanted to check on the new family.

But the mother and father swan were honking desperately. Their babies had wandered away and were lost!

"Don't worry," Briar Rose told the swans. "We'll find them."

"They were probably hungry," said Flora. But there were no swan babies in the bushes, because swans don't eat berries.

Fauna thought the babies might have gone exploring. But swans don't climb trees.

And Merryweather learned that the baby swans definitely were *not* in the mud patch.

Briar Rose thought about where young swans might want to go. Somewhere warm? Somewhere comfortable?

Briar Rose found the young swans safe
and warm, napping in a patch of soft,
sunny grass near the pond.

Everyone felt pleased and happy. After all, there's nothing like a beautiful spring day and the warmth of new friendships.

Princesses through the Seasons
Winter

Rapunzel's Winter Adventure

One morning, Rapunzel woke up thrilled to find the entire forest covered in a sparkling blanket of snow. She dashed to her window, leaned out and let the snowflakes land on her nose.

Pascal wanted
Rapunzel to play in
the snow.

"You know I can't go
outside, Pascal," she
said.

So Pascal did his best to bring the magic of winter to Rapunzel. He brought her bright red berries that she strung into garlands.

When he pointed to the frost on the windowpane, Rapunzel was so enchanted that she painted snowflakes on the wall.

Soon Rapunzel brought Pascal by
the fire and knitted him a cozy sweater.

A year later, Rapunzel was no longer enjoying winter from her tower. She was jumping in the snow, making snowmen and going on wild sleigh rides with Flynn, Max and Pascal. Rapunzel discovered she loved winter inside... and out!

Snowflakes in Agrabah

One day, Aladdin surprised Jasmine with a trip to a winter wonderland. Jasmine loved the snow. Abu was afraid at first, but soon found out he could have lots of fun with the frosty stuff!

Jasmine laughed as Abu
made a snowman that
looked just like him!

She loved Magic Carpet's
snow angels, too.

But most of all, she loved
the fun they had together.

As they warmed up by a cozy fire, Jasmine wished they could bring some winter fun to Agrabah.

When they returned home, Jasmine had a wonderful idea. They could make snowflakes and turn the palace into a winter wonderland!

Jasmine and Aladdin hung
paper snowflakes everywhere.
Soon, the palace was as white as
a snowy forest.

Jasmine smiled. Her wish came
true. They brought winter fun to
everyone!

Enchanted Winter Party

One snowy day, Belle and the Beast came up with a plan to have a surprise party for all the enchanted objects. They wanted to thank them for their hard work.

Mrs Potts, Cogsworth and Lumiere saw the
happy couple whispering and thought it would be
lovely to host a surprise tea party for them!

Belle and the Beast walked through the snowy forest gathering decorations for the party. Belle found holly berries and the Beast gathered frosty pine cones.

Meanwhile in the kitchen, Mrs Potts
was busy brewing tea for their surprise party!
Lumiere and Cogsworth even managed to
bake some festive cakes.

Belle decorated the parlour with holly as the Beast wrapped tiny presents.

Belle smiled. The room was finally ready for the party!

Just then, the enchanted objects brought in tea and cakes and shouted, "Surprise!"

Everyone laughed and enjoyed the wonderful winter party they made for each other.

The Snow Dwarfs

One snowy winter day, Snow White said to the Prince, "I think we should visit the Dwarfs' cottage. I'm sure they'd enjoy some hot soup on a cold day."

Snow White opened the cottage door. The Dwarfs were not home. "They're probably off to work," she said and happily began to prepare the soup.

But soon, Snow White began to worry.
"Perhaps we should look for them," she said.
"They're very little men and the snow is
very deep."

When they reached the mine, Snow
White gasped. There stood seven little
frozen men!

Suddenly, Happy rushed from the mine.
"How do you like our snowmen?"

"You mean snow-Dwarfs!"
Grumpy said.
Everyone laughed and headed
back to their cottage.

Once they were home, they all enjoyed
some good soup to warm their tummies
and good company to warm their hearts.

Rapunzel and the Golden Rule

*R*apunzel was about to see her lifelong dream come true! She had just ventured out of her tall tower for the very first time. A young man named Flynn was taking her to the Kingdom to see the floating lights that appeared in the sky every year on her birthday. Unfortunately, a horse named Maximus appeared – and tried to drag Flynn away!

Flynn had stolen something from the palace and the palace horse Maximus was determined to arrest him. Luckily, Rapunzel persuaded Maximus to let Flynn go – at least until after she had seen the floating lights. But when Flynn tried to climb onto Maximus's back, the horse threw him into the mud!

"I don't like this horse," Flynn said. "And this horse doesn't like me."

Rapunzel was sure she could teach Flynn and Maximus to like each other. But she knew it wasn't going to be easy....

Rapunzel explained the golden rule to Flynn and Maximus. To get along, they needed to treat each other in the same way that they themselves would like to be treated. That meant they had to be nice to each other! To demonstrate, Rapunzel scratched Maximus's ears.

"See?" she asked Flynn. "Now you do it."

Flynn reluctantly patted Maximus on the head. Rapunzel was thrilled that they were getting along better already.

"Now let's all go to the Kingdom together," she said.

Entering the kingdom was a little tricky, since Flynn was wanted by the palace guards. But Maximus let the young man hide behind him as they walked past the guards. Flynn was very grateful for the horse's help.

That day, Maximus kept a
sharp eye on Flynn so that he
wouldn't try to escape. The
horse was surprised when he saw
the young man being kind to
Rapunzel and the animals of the
kingdom.

And soon Maximus
began to realize that
maybe Flynn wasn't so
bad after all....

Later that evening, something terrible happened. Rapunzel was taken away and locked up in her hidden tower! Flynn and Maximus knew they had to work together to rescue her.

Working as a team, Maximus and Flynn found the hidden tower – and saved their friend Rapunzel!

Unfortunately, during the escape, Rapunzel's long golden hair was cut off. But she had gained something new – two wonderful friends. And Flynn and Maximus had finally learned the golden rule – thanks to Rapunzel!

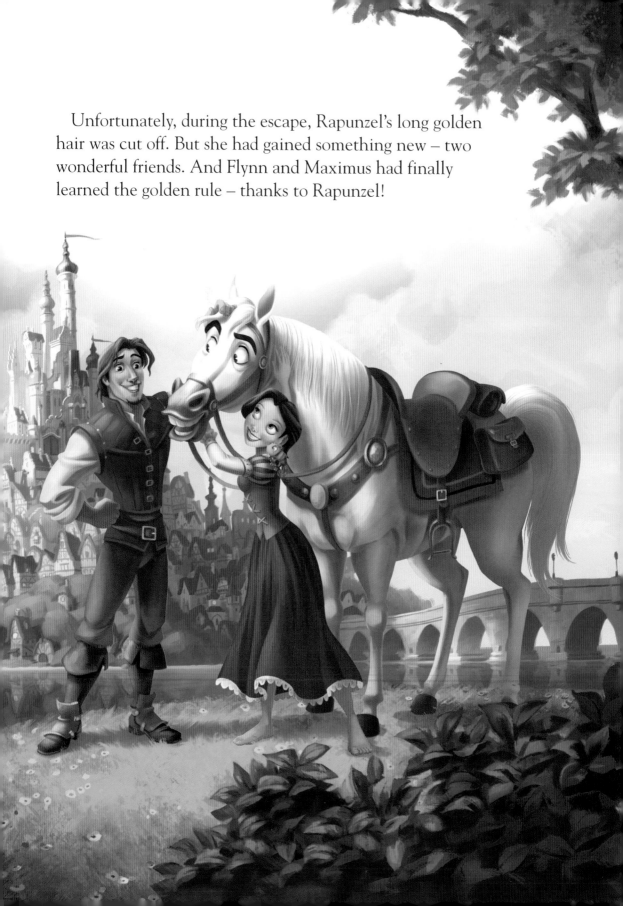

Jasmine and the Two Tigers

One morning, Princess Jasmine and her pet tiger, Rajah, were riding through the busy streets of Agrabah. They came upon a big, colourful circus tent that had been put up the night before. The tiger's eyes opened wide as he stared at the circus poster.

"That looks like fun," Jasmine said to Rajah. "But we really should be going. It's almost time for lunch."

Back at the palace, the tiger hardly touched his food.
"What do you think is wrong with Rajah?" Jasmine asked.
Aladdin shrugged. "Maybe a nice long carriage ride would
make him feel better," he suggested.

"Yes, let's do that right after we finish eating," Jasmine said.

Soon Jasmine, Aladdin, Abu and Rajah were riding through Agrabah in the royal carriage. As they rolled past the circus poster, the tiger suddenly perked up.

"Hmmm," Aladdin said. "Maybe we should take Rajah to the circus."

Inside the circus tent, the announcer said, "I now present
Mallika – the star of our show!" And out walked a beautiful tigress.
Jasmine saw Rajah's face light up. He was in love!

When the show was over, Jasmine and Aladdin took Rajah to meet
Mallika. The two tigers were very happy to be together – and clearly did
not want to be apart.

"Can Mallika please come live at my palace?" Jasmine asked the circus
owner. "She would be very happy there."

"I'm sorry, Mallika is our star," the owner replied. "Without her, there
wouldn't be a circus."

The next day at the palace, Rajah was miserable.
Jasmine had the royal animal keeper bring in other
tigers to keep Rajah company.

But none of them could take the place of Mallika.

That night, there was a knock at the palace door. It was the circus owner – and a very sad-looking tigress.

"Ever since Rajah left the circus, Mallika won't eat," the circus owner said. "Even though she's the star of my show, I want her to be happy. So I've come to give her to you."

The two tigers ran to each other and gently touched noses.

Jasmine and Aladdin were very happy for Rajah and Mallika. But they felt bad for the circus owner. Without his star tigress, the circus would surely close.

Suddenly, Jasmine had a wonderful idea....

The very next morning, the circus tent was moved right next to Jasmine's palace! Mallika could perform at the royal circus every day and come home to Rajah every evening.

A royal ball was held to celebrate. And everyone – Jasmine and Aladdin, the circus owner and the two tigers – lived happily ever after.

I finished
this book on

• •